For Murray, the wave rider

www.dragonbloodpirates.co.uk

ORCHARD BOOKS
338 Euston Road, London NW1 3BH

First published in 2008 by Lothian Children's Books,
an imprint of Hachette Livre Australia
First published in the UK in 2010 by Orchard Books

ISBN 978 1 40830 742 7

A CIP catalogue record for this book is available from the British Library.

10 9 8 7 6 5 4 3 2 1

Printed in Great Britain by J F Print Ltd., Sparkford

Orchard Books is a division of Hachette Children's Books,
an Hachette UK company.

www.hachette.co.uk

Treasure and Trouble

Dan Jerris

N

W

E

S

Death Islan

Shipwreck Island

Cannibal Island

abre Island

Town

Dragon's Stomach

Snake Island

Ghost Island

Dragon Blood Islands

Pirate Mateys and Scallywags

Alleric (Al) Breas: Lives in Drake Drive and owns a mysterious sea trunk that takes him to the Dragon Blood Islands.

Jack Seabrook: Al's best friend.

Blacktooth McGee: A very nasty pirate who runs the brigantine *The Revenge.*

Flash Johnny: Blacktooth's devious and greedy cabin boy.

Snakeboot: A magical white three-legged cat with purple eyes. Legend has it he once belonged to a terrifying pirate called Vicious Victor.

Pigface McNurt: Blacktooth's bosun; a massive pirate with a ring through his nose.

Snotty Nell: A horrible one-eyed pirate who sails a frigate called *The Tormentor.*

Grenda: Snotty Nell's daughter.

Sharkbait: Snotty Nell's one-legged bosun.

Vampire Zu: Snotty Nell's huge first mate.

Gunner: The pirate captain of the ship *The Booty.*

Mozzy: *The Booty*'s bosun (petty officer).

Slicer: *The Booty*'s cook.

Mahoot: Captain Gunner's cabin boy.

Grandfather: Mahoot's grandfather and guardian of the swimming elephants on Sabre Island.

Stanley Spong: A crooked, sneaky trader who cheats people.

Vicious Victor: A pirate ghost. He used to pillage the Dragon Blood Islands and he stole Prince Alleric's magical sabre.

Prince Alleric: The prince who once ruled Sabre Island but disappeared in mysterious circumstances.

Halimeda (Hally) Breas: Al's younger sister.

Greeny Joe: A shark so big and old that mould grows on his skin, making him glow green in the dark.

Kidnapped

Alleric Breas looked around in surprise. He was in a small room filled with barrels and boxes. There were no windows, but a dim light came through large cracks in the door. His sister, Hally, squeezed his hand tightly in apprehension.

Just then Jack Seabrook, Al's best friend, began to appear. He shimmered, mist-like, then solidified. In his arms was their three-legged, purple-eyed pirate cat, Snakeboot.

They heard wind roaring in the rigging and waves crashing against a wooden hull, followed by the strong smell of seawater and oilcloth.

"Do you think we're in the cabin of a ship sailing through the Dragon Blood Islands?" Jack asked.

Al glanced around. "It's too small for a cabin. By the look of all the boxes here, I'd say we're in some sort of storeroom."

"I'll try the door," said Jack. "I'll peek out and see where we've landed this time."

The trio had just arrived from number five Drake Drive, in the twenty-first century. Only minutes before, the boys had gone into Al's attic, where they'd found Hally waiting for them, dressed in her princess clothes, ready to visit the Dragon Blood Islands. The boys then changed into their sea-going pirate clothes, and Jack belted on the pirate sword he'd found on Cannibal Island. Al took Hally's hand and unlocked their old sea trunk. He put the key in his pocket, opened the lid, and together they stepped inside.

Jack picked up Snakeboot and followed. Within seconds they had vanished from the attic.

The boys had hoped to return to Cannibal Island, where they'd previously left Captain Gunner and his pirate crew, but instead they found themselves inside the storeroom of a sailing ship.

The ship tacked suddenly and Hally lost her balance and fell over. Jack clutched at the door and gave it a push. "Door's locked," he said.

Al lifted the lid of a barrel and checked inside. "It's gunpowder," he said.

"I hope this is the storeroom on *The Booty*," said Jack.

"We could see if it's Captain Gunner's ship by looking for the sapphires and rubies he stole from those poor tribes people on Cannibal Island," suggested Al.

"Does Captain Gunner really have

sapphires and rubies?" asked Hally, brightening at the mention of jewels.

"Loads of them," replied Jack, "and if this is *The Booty*'s storeroom, then they might be in here."

"We should look around anyway," said Al. "It'll give us a clue as to what ship we've landed in. Luckily we didn't land on a rock with that horrible shark, Greeny Joe, trying to eat us."

"Shark?" cried Hally. "You never told me about any shark."

"He's huge," said Jack, enjoying Hally's look of fear, "with massive teeth. Greeny Joe's covered in green mould, so he glows in the dark. He chewed up Snotty Nell."

"Greeny Joe's got a real thing for Snotty," added Al. "She smells like a big Christmas pudding and Greeny Joe follows her everywhere trying to get another bite."

Hally shivered as she remembered

the horrible pirate who'd kidnapped the elephants on Sabre Island. "Snotty's a nasty old grouch," she said, "but it must be awful to have a shark following you around all the time, trying to eat you." She took a small step towards a cupboard and opened it. A carved wooden chest sitting high up on a shelf caught her eye. "What do you think's in *that*?" she said, standing on tiptoes, but she was too small to reach. "I can't get it."

Al reached up and pulled at the chest. "It's heavy," he grunted as he brought it down. When he opened the lid Hally gasped in surprise as glittering blue and red gems glowed in the darkened room.

"So many!" she cried. "Are they real?"

"Yes, they are," said Jack, inspecting the treasure. "So now we've worked out we're on Gunner's ship, how will we explain how we got here, and with Hally?"

Al shrugged. Captain Gunner would never believe they just sneaked on board and locked themselves in the ship's storeroom.

"Can I keep some of the jewels?" asked Hally, oblivious to the problem at hand. She fingered the gems and rolled a few of them in the palm of her hand.

"They're cursed," Jack told her.

Hally dropped the jewels immediately. "Are they?" she asked. "I don't believe you."

"I'm serious. A deadman's curse," said Jack. "If these jewels aren't used for good, someone will steal them."

"You have to give them away for a good cause," explained Al, "and although Captain Gunner gave away most of the jewels he found, he couldn't help himself and stole these."

As Al spoke, *The Booty* tacked again and the children were tossed to one side of the small room. The treasure chest tipped over, spilling the gems across the floor. They had just begun to pick them up when they heard a cannon being fired, followed by another hard tack.

"Oh, no, we're being attacked," cried Jack. "Get down low."

Al, Jack and Hally sat on the floor and waited anxiously as musket fire and yelling thundered around them. Shortly afterwards the grinding of wood on wood and a deafening crunch told them they had collided with another ship. They heard the sails billowing and flapping as *The Booty* was hauled into the breeze, followed by the screams and shouts of a sword fight. They listened in fear to the war cries of the boarding pirates.

"If the invaders win," said Al, "they'll head straight for this storeroom."

"I hope it's not Blacktooth," declared

Jack. "I don't think he'd be a happy man after having his fort blown up."

"Snotty's not too keen on us either," said Al, "but I'd rather it was her. She's got a child of her own so I doubt she'd kill us."

"Oh!" wailed Hally. "I only wanted to play princesses; I didn't want to get killed!"

Her words had barely left her mouth when the storeroom door burst open and Snotty Nell, waving a sabre, pushed her way into the room. Her one good eye flashed with the fire of battle. When it fell upon the pile of jewels it flashed with the fire of greed. "Who'd have thought old Gunner would have such riches?" she roared. "Sneaky old fool." When she saw the children she took a step back. She wiped a long green booger from her scarred nose. "And who'd think he'd have three children locked up in the storeroom?" She peered at Hally. "A girl!"

Treasure and Trouble

"A princess," said Hally. "Princess Halimeda."

Al's eyebrows shot up at Hally's words.

"A princess, are you?" snarled Snotty Nell. "Then that box of jewels would explain a lot. That must be your ransom payment." She turned on Al and Jack. "And you two rapscallions, you have robbed me of a diamond, and you owe me!" She took an angry step towards Jack and shook her sabre.

Jack reached for the sword in his belt. Quick as a viper, Snotty grabbed his hand, pulled the sword away and tossed it behind her, pushing Jack to the floor. Al jumped to his feet to defend his friend, but Snotty grasped his shirt collar with her free hand and shook him angrily.

"Leave my brother alone!" Hally cried, then burst into tears.

"Oh? A brother?" growled Snotty. She stared hard at Al. "So the truth comes out." She turned her attention back to Jack. "You must be a royal too, or you wouldn't be locked up in here with these two. It explains why Gunner had you two on board last time. He was waiting for his ransom payment." Finally she put her sabre in its scabbard. "Vampire!" she bellowed.

A huge pirate appeared and leered at the children, baring his sharp-pointed teeth.

"Tie this lot up," Snotty said. "Don't harm them, but you know how tricky these boys can be, so put them in sacks where they can't wriggle free. We'll take them on board our ship with their lovely treasure." She pointed to the jewels spilled across the room.

"And when you three are on board, we'll put you to work," sneered Vampire Zu as he bound Al's hands together. "It'll do rich little smarty-pants like you a bit of good to work hard for the likes of us."

Minutes later, Hally, Jack and Al were trussed like turkeys, covered with large flour bags and hoisted onto the backs of Snotty's pirates to be taken on board her ship, *The Tormentor.*

The Curse of the Jewels

Al, Jack and Hally found themselves on the aft deck with Snotty Nell, her one-legged bosun, Sharkbait, and her first mate, Vampire Zu.

"These children are royals," Snotty explained to them, "so when we get to town we'll see Stanley Spong about getting some more gold and jewels from their rich parents. But while they are on board, they should be working, and working hard."

"They can scrub the decks," suggested Vampire Zu.

"Not in my good dress," said Hally, putting on her demanding voice.

"You're right, my lady," said Snotty. "You certainly can't work in such fine clothes."

Hally beamed happily. The boys were shocked by Snotty's kindness.

But Snotty hadn't finished. "You can take off your smart clothes and put on one of my daughter's old smocks. And you can be Grenda's servant girl, Miss 'I'm-a-princess'. You'll do everything Grenda says or you won't get a bite to eat."

It wasn't long before Al and Jack found themselves with scrubbing brushes, slopping vinegar on the decks. "I hope that treasure hurries up and does its curse thing," said Al. "I don't want to be here too long."

"And there's no way we can escape,"

said Jack. "All the pirates are watching us like hawks."

After many hours of hard work, the boys were allowed to sit in the shade and have a drink. While they were recovering, Grenda and Hally sauntered over.

"So," said Grenda, "your sister's a bit odd. She wants to play something stupid called

'popstars'. I don't understand a word she says, to be honest. What sort of stars go pop? What sort of game could that be?"

"You sing," said Hally crossly. "I told you! You sing popular songs, like the ones on the radio."

"See what I mean?" said Grenda. She leant over to Al and whispered, "Is she

all right in the head? You know, is the poor thing a bit...well...touched by the sun?"

Al looked at his sister. "Hmm, she is a bit," he replied.

"And," said Grenda, "she says the fantastic treasure we got off silly old Gunner isn't your parents' treasure after all."

"That's right," said Jack.

"And what's more, it's cursed," said Al. "If your mum doesn't give it away quickly to do help someone else, she'll be robbed herself."

Grenda laughed. "Goodness me, you two will say anything. I think the treasure did belong to you. You're trying to trick me. Mum says you were locked in the storeroom with it, and you're rich."

"No," said Al, "we found it on Cannibal Island and Gunner stole some of it, even though the curse said he'd lose it if—"

"Rubbish," interrupted Grenda. "I don't

want to listen to any more of your nonsense. Mum's right. You're just a load of big heads who put the likes of us down." She turned to Hally. "And I'm sick of you, too, so you can scrub the deck." Grenda handed Hally a scrubbing brush and flounced off.

Hally held the brush and looked absolutely miserable, but before she could utter a word of complaint, a cry came from the lookout in the crow's nest above. "Sail, sail!"

Hally, Jack and Al turned and looked out over the ocean. Just off starboard a two-masted brigantine flying the Jolly Roger was racing across the water and closing in on them fast. "It's Blacktooth!" cried Al. "Now we're in for it."

Since she was not expecting another battle so soon, Snotty Nell was running *The Tormentor* before the breeze. Even with all her sails billowing, Blacktooth's ship gained on her and fired a cannon across her bows. Snotty hove to and re-armed her tired crew with pistols and swords, ready for battle.

As *The Revenge* came alongside, Blacktooth was standing on the prow. "You owe me a treassure," he hissed, "and if

you can't pay me back, I'm ssinking you on the sspot!"

"Just try," Snotty snarled. "I'll have your guts for garters!"

Under cover of his men's musket shots, Blacktooth leapt from the prow with a hop, step and flying jump, and landed on the gunnels of *The Tormentor.* His heavily armed men swarmed onto the quarterdeck with grappling hooks. Snotty Nell's crew attacked and a sword fight broke out. Vampire Zu lunged with two sabres swinging, and Blacktooth fired one of his pistols, hitting Vampire Zu in the backside. The huge pirate dived with a scream into the rigging. "Got you, you thief!" cried Blacktooth. "That's for losing my treassure last time!"

Al and Jack grabbed Hally and raced for cover amid the acrid smoke of pistol and cannon fire.

Within minutes it was all over. Snotty Nell had not been prepared for battle and Blacktooth had his sword at her throat. Pinning her against the missen mast, he demanded, "Give up! Tell your cowardly crew to lay down their weaponss."

Blacktooth then seized the treasure Snotty had taken from Gunner. He lined *The Tormentor*'s crew along the poop deck and he and his cabin boy, Flash, removed any jewellery they found on them. They took an earring from Vampire, a gold chain from Snotty and a bracelet from Grenda.

When Blacktooth got to Al he stopped and glared. "You!" he scowled. "You took my emerald." He raised his sabre in a violent rage. Al held his gaze. He would not let Blacktooth think he was a coward by ducking or cringing.

Blacktooth glared viciously for a second longer, then looked along the line of

captured pirates. "Flash, what do you think we should do with thiss lot?"

Flash smiled his false toothy smile, but then a cold, hateful smirk darkened his face. "Make them suffer," he said. "Scupper the ship!"

"What a good idea," said Blacktooth. "Heave down the ssails and tosss them over the sside with the ship'ss wheel," he ordered. While his men disabled the ship he smiled so broadly that he showed his one rotting black tooth.

Blacktooth's crew then boarded *The Revenge*, eased their ship away from the *The Tormentor* and sailed to starboard with a cannon aimed at *The Tormentor*'s hull. Letting out a smoking roar, the shot tore into the wooden hull, splintering it just below the sea line. Water poured into the hold.

Blacktooth laughed heartily as he waved

goodbye. Pointing down into the ocean, he yelled. "Greeny Joe'ss waiting for you! You'll never reach Davey Joness' locker before he getss you!"

Sure enough, circling the wounded ship was an enormous green shark.

Hally clung to her brother's arm and sobbed. "I want to go home!"

"Shut up," snapped Grenda. "Being a blubbering baby won't help us."

"Grenda's right," soothed Al, patting his sister's hand. "We'll need to be brave if we want to survive."

The Tormentor drifted for several hours. Everyone ran with bailing buckets to and from the leaking hull. The boys puffed up and down the stairs as they gathered and emptied the buckets. Hally and Grenda worked quickly, filling the buckets and passing them to the nearest pirate.

The Tormentor was blown by the wind and

pulled by the currents. The starboard wind meant that the ship listed away from the sea, helping to slow the gushing water. But if they were tempted to stop bailing, even for a moment, they only had to look into the ocean at the circling shark to see what would happen if they gave up.

Even Vampire Zu, who had bandaged his aching bum, bailed bucket after bucket of

water, tirelessly handing them to the waiting crew. He lifted Hally to a drier position as the water began to rise.

After a few exhausting hours, and just before *The Tormentor* was about to sink forever, an island appeared on the horizon. "Lower the longboat and attach a tow-rope," ordered Snotty. "We'll pull *The Tormentor* aground and fix her up."

With great effort the pirates did as she commanded, rowing the sinking ship towards shore. As they approached the beach, several masts became visible. Then the skeletons of other ships darkened the shoreline. "Now, *there's* a spot of luck," said Snotty. "We've come upon Shipwreck Bay." She grinned and wiped away a dribble of snot from her top lip. "There'll be sails and timber, wheels and wood. We can fix our ship in no time."

Finally they ran *The Tormentor*'s keel into the sand and, when they were sure they were aground, Snotty addressed the crew. "You lot worked like Trojans," she said. "I want to thank everyone. But now you must go ashore and look for material to repair the ship. Get to it!"

Shipwreck Island

Snotty Nell's crew fanned out across Shipwreck Island. It didn't take them long to find wood and a steering wheel, but a sail was a different matter. All the wrecks were missing sails and those that still hung from the masts had rotted or been shredded by the wind.

Al and Jack headed towards an old galleon. Its broken mast and decayed rigging hung over the deck and seaweed and bird droppings mouldered over its hull. Sand had washed around it with the tides, making a ramp from the shore to the hull. It was easy for the boys to climb aboard. Grenda and Hally followed some way behind.

Al found the captain's cabin with the door hanging from its hinges. He went inside and discovered that the room was in surprisingly good order. Jack stuck his head around the door. The captain's table and chair and the ship's log book were just as someone had left them. Al couldn't help but go straight to the

log book. He immediately turned to the last few pages. Jack joined him and, peering over his shoulder, began to read aloud:

Our cargo shifted in a storm, splintering our hull. We were forced before the wind and are wrecked on this island. We have run out of food and water, and now must take to our longboat and trust our seamanship as we row to sea. If we never return...

Jack turned to Al. "Now it goes all weird. Can you make it out?"

Al studied the next words:

Prncss Hlmd llrc's trsr s t hvy fr th lfbt. W hv brd t wth r sls n th slnd. Lk fr th cls, shld I nt rtrn.

"It's a simple code. You have to put in the vowels," explained Al. "It won't take long to figure out."

While the boys were working on the possible vowels to put in between the consonants, Grenda and Hally joined them. "What are you two wasting time with?" asked Grenda.

"We think the captain of this ship has buried some treasure and ship's stores," said Al. "He's left instructions written in code, and if he never came back to collect the treasure, then it might still be on this beach."

"Treasure?" Grenda took to her heels at the news, while Al continued to work on the code.

"I think it says it's Princess Halimeda Alleric's treasure," said Al, "but I can't be sure. It also says there are sails buried. We'd better go after Grenda and help them search."

At the news of treasure, Snotty Nell instantly set her men to digging, and while they worked, she ordered Sharkbait to bring her a cup of her favourite sahlep tea, made from orchid roots. As she sipped her honeyed drink on the quarterdeck, she averted her eyes from the ocean so, just for a moment, she could enjoy herself without seeing Greeny Joe's terrible fin cutting through the deeper water behind *The Tormentor.*

While all the pirates were digging in the sand, the children followed Al as he walked slowly down the beach. "The log book said to look for clues," he said, "so there must be some somewhere."

Jack, who had walked higher up on the beach, beckoned the others over. "Look, a tree with the code notched into it," he said. "It's almost too easy. See? *Dg hr.* That means 'Dig here'!"

Grenda ran off to get the pirates to help them, and it wasn't long before they unearthed a sea trunk. "It looks just like the trunk in your attic," Jack said to Al. "And look, it says 'Princess Halimeda' on the top."

"A treasure named after me!" cried Hally. "I can't wait to see it."

"Let's hope that when the pirates open it there *is* treasure inside," whispered Al. "I wouldn't want our attic to be full of pirates."

Jack raised his eyebrows at the horrible thought.

"Take the trunk back to the captain," ordered Vampire Zu. The men hauled it out of the sand and carried it away.

Al looked into the hole left by the trunk and saw a rope faintly visible in the sand. "Wait!" he called. "Vampire, wait! Look, there's something else buried here." He clambered down and pulled at the rope. Something heavy held it in place. He pulled as hard as he could, but nothing moved. Vampire Zu hobbled down into the hole beside Al and heaved on the rope with his large body.

"Sails!" cried Vampire, as he lifted a massive sail bag slowly out of the sand. "This boy has found us some sails!" He slapped Al so hard on the back that he was pushed face forward into the sand. Vampire Zu pulled the bag out with the help of the rest of the crew, who hoisted it onto their shoulders and headed back to *The Tormentor*.

Al climbed out of the hole and stood beside Jack.

"I think Vampire was being nice to you," said Jack, as Al brushed the sand off himself.

"I wonder what would happen if he was *really* nice," said Al.

Back on the deck of *The Tormentor*, Snotty opened the trunk. She pulled out a roll of silk cloth, bags of cooking spices, and then a diamond necklace, bracelet, tiara and several rings. There were also quite a few books, but Snotty threw them over the side in disgust. Then she pulled out a small bag filled with brooches. Some glittered with diamonds and pearls, but one brooch was a cameo, showing a painting of a girl with curly hair, wearing a crown. Snotty Nell looked at the picture and then at Hally.

"This looks strangely like you," she said.

Hally nodded. "It says it's my trunk," she said. "See?" she fingered the writing on the lid. "Princess Halimeda."

Snotty glared at the writing. "Hrmmph," she said. "Who cares? It's mine now. Tell you what, Your Highness, you can have your picture." She tossed the brooch to Hally, who pinned it on her smock.

Within a few days *The Tormentor* was fixed and ready to sail. The pirates hauled the ship out to sea on a high tide just before dawn, and with Greeny Joe still in pursuit, they sailed briskly out to sea. "We're hunting Blacktooth," said Snotty, as the wind filled the sails. "I want back what he stole and I want him to pay."

"He'll pay twice if I have it my way," growled Vampire Zu, rubbing his rump.

"I want us geared up for battle," Snotty ordered. "No one is taking us by surprise again. Prime the cannons. Clean your swords and guns. That barnacle brain is going to wish he'd never been born." The crew set to work immediately. "And you boys," she added, turning to Al and Jack, "since you found the sails, I'll let you off scrubbing the decks. You can go below and help the cook make a celebratory dinner.

Tell him to double-dose it with salted mackerel, onions and mangoes, loads of liver and the octopus we caught yesterday. It's salmagundi for dinner tonight!"

The Scourge of Greeny Joe

Late in the afternoon, Al and Jack brought a steaming cauldron of salmagundi onto *The Tormentor*'s deck and placed it near the day cabin. The cauldron had a fixed lid so the stinking stew wouldn't spill in the heavy swell. Al shuddered as he lifted the lid and ladled the first bowl. He took the lumpy brown concoction to Vampire Zu, who stood at the helm of the ship, armed and ready for a fight. He took the bowl without looking at Al, lifted it to his lips and gulped down the steaming mess. "Bring us another," he declared, smacking his lips. "Ah, it's the best ever. Thank the chef, then take a bowl to the captain."

Al shook his head, bewildered. "How can they eat this stuff?" he muttered to himself. "I've never smelt anything so awful in my life!"

He was just about to pour the next bowl of stew from the cauldron when he heard a familiar cry. "Sail! Batten down the hatches!" cried Vampire Zu. "We have our prey in sight."

As Jack secured the lid on the prized pirate stew, he asked, "Is there going to be another fight?" His eyes were big with excitement.

Al nodded. "Nothing'll stop Snotty getting back at Blacktooth."

Joining Vampire at the helm, Snotty

put a spyglass to her eye. "It's Blacktooth and Gunner," she cried. "And they're already fighting!"

As they closed in on their quarry, Al could clearly see the puffs of gunshot smoke and *The Booty* and *The Revenge* locked together in battle. Realising things were about to get dangerous, he called out to Snotty, "Where are the girls?"

"Down in my cabin," she replied, with her eye fixed on her hated enemies. "And told to stay there!"

Snotty closed in on Blacktooth and Gunner. She manoeuvred the ship so it sailed in on a port tack and broadsided Blacktooth, ramming him between herself and Gunner. The ships shuddered under the impact and wood splintered from the gunnels. The heaving swell tossed the ships this way and that. Gunner's ship swung aft and was caught behind *The Tormentor* so it abutted the sterns of the two ships.

Shocked by the sudden assault and flaying his cat-o'-nine-tails whip, Blacktooth turned some of his men towards Snotty's ship. With the large swells it was difficult for the men to attack. The ships rose and fell, as muskets were fired and smoke swirled across the decks.

On one giant wave, Gunner's men leapt onto the stern of Blacktooth's ship, clambered up the masts and began to chop at the rigging. Some of Blacktooth's men swarmed into the rigging to defend it and hurled themselves at the attacking men. Blacktooth brought a smouldering caldron of hot coals onto the deck, and seconds later his men were throwing great globs of burning tar at *The Tormentor.* The tar caught on the wooden decks just in front of Al and Jack.

Seeing the danger, Al took off his frockcoat and beat at the flames. Jack

grabbed a bucket and hauled water up from the tossing seas. As they were dousing the fire Al turned to find several of Blacktooth's pirates running along their deck. They were loading and firing their muskets as they jumped on board.

With bloodcurdling yells, Snotty's pirates locked together with them, wielding their swords in a mighty hand-to-hand battle. In the middle of it all, Hally and Grenda climbed out through a hatch from below deck and looked around, terrified.

Al dodged and weaved through the fighting men, ducking the sharp blades, then grabbed his sister and pushed her flat. "Get back down below or you'll be killed!" he shouted. Hally and Grenda needed no further warning. With tears of fright, the girls vanished back down the stairs. Al dodged back through the fighting men and reached the relative safety of the day cabin behind the steering wheel to rejoin Jack.

Snotty also came onto the steerage deck. "Oil!" she shrieked. "Oil! Make it slippery so Blacktooth can't board so easily." At once her men tipped oil onto the gunnels and the deck nearby.

In the meantime, Gunner, still hard-up against the sterns of his enemies' ships, was causing havoc on Blacktooth's ship. His men were hanging from the rigging on *The Revenge* and they had chopped so hard at the halyards and mainstays that the ship's masts were swaying dangerously. Cut ropes swung down onto the decks and tangled people as they fought. One of the yards crashed onto the deck, scattering Blacktooth's crew.

While Blacktooth was besieged by Gunner's men, Vampire Zu jumped aboard *The Revenge* and, with a group of men behind him, battled his way to the storeroom. They soon returned with Snotty's stolen treasure.

Watching his treasure vanishing aboard *The Tormentor*, Blacktooth roared with anger and leapt after it. His feet touched Snotty's deck but he began to slip in the oil. Snotty, seeing the advantage, raced towards him with her sword held high. Down she sliced, cutting her enemy. Blacktooth stepped back, holding his bloodied cheek, and fled to *The Revenge.*

Snotty ran after him, but she miscalculated. Slipping on the oily gunnels, she lost her balance and, below her, Greeny Joe lifted his head and opened his great jaws. Snotty's scream pierced the air. The pirates stopped fighting and watched as she fell and spiralled downwards.

Centimetres from the water, Snotty grabbed a loose line from Blacktooth's ship. The shark jumped out of the water, just as Snotty pulled herself, hand over hand, out of his reach.

Greeny Joe missed her by millimetres. Everyone watching felt the clash of his empty jaws. The shark fell back into the water with a splash. Again he leapt, but now Snotty was well up the side of the hull, still climbing the rope. The gigantic swell rocked the ships, so on every second wave Snotty was sent back towards the water and Greeny Joe thrashed again and again.

Blacktooth, seeing his opportunity to rid himself of Snotty Nell once and for all, slashed at the rope she was climbing. Vampire Zu grabbed a ship hook, hooked the other end of Snotty's rope

and pulled it onto *The Tormentor,* just as Blacktooth cut through it above her.

Snotty fell towards the ocean once again. A howling gust of wind whipped at all the ships and tipped them, just as the swell pushed them, and Snotty was dunked head first into the water. As Greeny Joe leapt again at his prey, Vampire Zu hauled with all his might. The ships swung back and Snotty, still hanging onto the rope, popped out of the water, her eye bulging in terror.

Seeing his long-hunted prey escaping, Greeny made a colossal leap, just as Vampire Zu pulled Snotty onto *The Tormentor.* She clutched the slippery rails and hauled herself over. At that moment the ships rolled lower in the swell and the shark landed just behind Snotty with a mighty crash.

Everyone fled except for Snotty, who slipped and slid backwards towards the shark. At that moment Grenda and Hally came back up from below decks. Grenda, seeing her mother in such danger, screamed in fear. Snotty wailed in terror and the great beast thrashed his tail, his massive eyes fixed on his pirate prey.

Wet, and on an oily deck, Snotty tried to take a couple of steps forward, but she slipped and fell again, right beside Al. Greeny Joe flipped towards her. The giant beast was only centimetres away.

The ship tipped again and Snotty began to slide backwards towards the shark. Greeny Joe opened his mouth wide.

Al thought quickly. Right beside him was the salmagundi. He lifted the lid of the cauldron and tossed the hot stinking mess, as hard as he could, into the shark's mouth.

The Big Vomit

Greeny Joe swallowed and shut his powerful jaws, as Snotty finally managed to get to her feet and scramble away.

The huge creature convulsed as the stew fermented inside him. Hally and Grenda moved cautiously up beside Al, as Greeny Joe twisted in agony.

The shark's eyes rolled, his great mouth opened and Al could see his terrifying double row of teeth. A great gurgling came from his belly. Not one pirate moved as the shark's massive tail flayed about in a frenzy, smashing the aft end of *The Tormentor* and breaking down the gunnels. From the rails of *The Booty*, Gunner peered down at the agonised shark.

Grenda cried, "You've killed it! Hooray!"

Suddenly, Greeny Joe stopped thrashing. He shuddered. His stomach heaved and a terrible bubbling roar came from his gizzard. A massive cloud of bright green vomit sloshed up in the air and out over the decks.

It covered Al, Snotty and Vampire. It coated Gunner from head to foot, and dripped all over *The Booty*'s deck.

Then the great shark convulsed and vomited again. Great globules of green goo sloshed over the sails. With one final extraordinary thrash of his tail, he broke through the starboard rail on Snotty's ship and threw himself into the ocean.

Al also saw his chance. He grabbed his little sister by the hand. "Jack!" he whispered. "Run! Run and jump onto Gunner's ship!"

Together the three dashed for safety. With the aid of a huge swell, they leapt across the gap between the fighting pirate ships and landed with a sliding skid on *The Booty*'s deck.

Return of the Idol's Eye

Snotty Nell had had enough for one day. With her treasure back on board, and the shark back in the ocean, she ordered a fast retreat. Gunner also disengaged *The Booty* and with the children safe on board, he turned and fled. Blacktooth couldn't follow as the rigging on *The Revenge* was in tatters.

Minutes later, Al, Jack and Hally were greeted by Mahoot, the cabin boy, and their friend Slicer, the cook. "We thought we'd lost you forever," said Slicer. "One minute you were with us on Cannibal Island, and then you were gone. We thought you were dead."

"Snotty Nell got us," said Hally. "She took me away in a sack."

"Well, we're glad you're safe," said Gunner. "But the mystery is, we found your cat on our ship. He must have snuck aboard and hid after Snotty kidnapped you from Cannibal Island."

As Gunner spoke, Snakeboot appeared and rubbed himself around Al's legs.

"Snotty dropped your sword, young Mr Seabrook," added Slicer. "I've been keeping it safe for you." He handed Jack his prized pirate sword.

"We knew Snotty had to have kidnapped you when we found this," said Gunner. "So we decided we were gunner get you back. We were searching for you when Blacktooth

found us. He wasn't too happy about his fort blowing sky high, so he went for us."

"What a mess we're in," said Hally, looking at her clothes.

Al stood there in his burnt frockcoat, covered in Greeny Joe's vomit.

"Yes," said Gunner, also dripping in green slime. "*The Booty*'s a disaster too after all that fighting. How about we clean the ship and then we clean ourselves?"

Everyone set to scrubbing and washing down the deck, as well as making repairs. Gunner, however, took Hally below and made sure Slicer gave her some 'figgy doody' (which Al later found out was pirate cake).

While Hally was being treated like a princess, Al grabbed a bucket of water and threw it at a sail. A great glob of green goo fell to the deck. He pushed it with a broom towards the scuppers. Something glinted in the sunlight. Al reached over and looked closely. "The elephant's emerald eye!" he cried. He held a huge sparkling emerald in his hands. Everyone rushed to his side.

Mahoot reached out for it. "We must take it to Grandfather," he said happily. "Sabre Island will have its powers back!"

Captain Gunner took the emerald from Mahoot and held it up high so the sun shone through it. "Ahhh," he sighed. "What I'd do if I had this to sell." A momentary glimmer of greed came to his eyes, but it faded. "It's brought no one any good," he said. "And it should be with Mahoot's grandfather, to protect the elephants." He turned to the crew. "Set sail for Sabre Island," he commanded. "We're gunner look for treasure in Alleric Castle."

The Cameo Code

When they arrived on Sabre Island, the children headed to the elephant temple and handed the emerald to Mahoot's grandfather. His eyes danced with light as he placed the missing emerald in the golden elephant idol's empty eye socket. The emerald, now returned to its rightful place, burned with a fierce radiance.

"Thanks to you," said Mahoot's grandfather, "the idol has two eyes once again. If anyone comes to hurt the elephants, the golden idol will be able to see them before they land. Then it will conjure up the magical storms of old and blow the bad people away." Mahoot's grandfather put a frail hand on Al's shoulders. "Since you came home, Prince Alleric, our island is becoming strong again. Its magical powers are returning. Now all Sabre Island needs is the Dragon Blood Sabre to return to its full glory. Do you think you can find it?"

"I don't know," said Al, humouring the old man, for ever since he'd visited Sabre Island, Mahoot's grandfather had believed him to be the lost Prince

Alleric, owner of the magical Dragon Blood Sabre.

"The ruby in the handle! Ah, how it glowed," said Mahoot's grandfather. "Made from a drop of dragon's blood, that is what the legend says. The ruby was found on this island, and a craftsman who knew the ancient magical ways forged the sabre over a dragon's fire. Three thousand folds of steel were in its blade. And the scabbard!" The old man smiled at Al. "Do you remember the scabbard?"

Al shook his head. "I'm afraid not," he said gently.

Mahoot's grandfather sighed. "I realise that since you went away you have forgotten much. The scabbard was made of fine chain mail decorated with four large diamonds. Legend says the diamonds were really the scales of the dragon, and when you wore your scabbard you were invincible."

Everyone's eyes widened at the amazing story. “I’d love to find it,” said Al, “but no one knows where it is and I don’t know where to look.”

“Remember the diary you had?” asked Mahoot's grandfather.

“Grandfather,” Mahoot interrupted. “Al isn’t the prince. You just think he looks like him. The prince would be around seventy years old if he were still alive.”

The old man ignored his grandson. “I kept it. I kept it for you,” he continued, patting Al on the shoulder. “I knew the right day would come.” He smiled up at the two magical emerald eyes now glimmering in the golden elephant idol’s head. “And you have proved to me that this is the right day.”

He went to the side of the temple and struggled with a huge earthenware pot, rolling it to one side. Underneath was

a rock-slab floor. Grandfather lifted one of the slabs and pulled out a book wrapped in silk. "This is the diary," he announced. He handed it to Al. "I cannot read. But you can. Perhaps there is a clue in here as to what your plans were before you left, and it might help you remember so you can go and find your wonderful sabre."

Al opened the book. He sat before the superb golden elephant and, in the soft light of the temple, with the scent of incense

giving out a hint of hidden mysteries, Al read the lost prince's diary aloud to his friends.

They sat entranced as the diary told them all about the magical powers of the great sabre and the wonderful parties held in Alleric Castle. Then came the terrible story of a time when Prince Alleric was away helping the elephants, and Vicious Victor, the pirate scourge of the Dragon Blood Islands, raided his castle. He stole Prince Alleric's sabre and a great deal of treasure.

Prince Alleric chased after Vicious Victor and had many battles with him, but never recovered his sabre. The sabre was actually useless to Victor because he didn't know the magical words that activated its powers. After hunting through the islands for many months, Prince Alleric returned. But when he came home he found disaster. Finally, Al read the last page.

My family is ruined! Four of my merchant ships have been sunk. We cannot pay the servants and the castle was raided while I was away. My poor sister, Halimeda, has done all she can, but a woman alone cannot defend a castle. I must send her to safety. I have created a special magic from my last treasure, a dragon's claw, and I have

sent her to a faraway place of safety with her last possessions in a sea trunk.

My dear friend who keeps the elephants has been loyal and brave, but it is too much even for him. I leave him my diary. I have one last place to go in search of the lost sabre. This place is heavily guarded. If I do not return, then my bones lie there.

"And that's where it ends," said Al, "except for the nice pattern around the last page. There's not one clue about where he went."

The children studied the diary's last page:

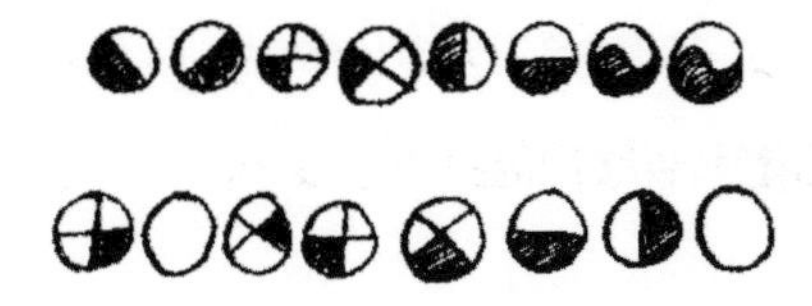

Hally examined her cameo, then passed it to Al. "On the back of the cameo," she said, "is a pattern a bit like the one in the diary."

"Is it a code?" asked Jack.

"It might be," said Al, inspecting the brooch. "There are a few shapes that are the same as in the diary. There are three groups of shapes on the cameo. If that means there are three words, does anyone have an idea what it might say?"

"It's *my* cameo," said Hally, tired of the boys fiddling with her brooch. "Can I have it back now?"

"You're a genius!" exclaimed Al. "It's your cameo! What if it says Princess Halimeda something or other? First, look for the vowels. If it does say Princess Halimeda, look for a vowel pattern."

"You're right," said Jack. "Where the 'I's should be, the patterns are the same. And so are the 'E's."

"Princess Halimeda Alleric!" cried Al. "Now we can work out the rest." Using sticks, Al and Jack quickly drew the patterns on the dusty floor and the corresponding letters below them. Pretty soon, the secret message in the diary was revealed.

"It says the sabre is on Ghost Island," Al told everyone. "We'll have to ask Gunner if he knows where that is – and if he'll take us there..."

Ghost Island

When Captain Gunner heard the boys' tale, he paled. "You don't expect me to go to Ghost Island, do you?" he said.

"The magical sabre might be there," said Al, "and there's masses of treasure, too."

"We all know there's treasure there," said Gunner. "But I'm not gunner go and neither are you. Only one man ever came back from those shores, and he was a gibbering mess. His hair went white overnight. He

went totally mad and ate his shoes."

"Please, Captain Gunner," begged Jack. "Isn't it worth a try?"

Gunner shook his head. "I'm setting sail tonight and we're heading for the outer islands. There are stories going around that rubies were found on an island and there's a shipment coming to town. We should go there now. We've wasted enough time here."

A few nights later, as the stars rose, Gunner set sail and they all went with him. The next day they sailed under a brisk southerly wind and made great time. A rain shower brought beautiful rainbows.

Captain Gunner came up on deck. "How about you boys climb the rigging?" he said. "Go up to the crow's nest and look for sail. We might come across that merchant ship full of rubies." He

handed Al a brass telescope.

Al and Jack had no intention of robbing any merchant ship, but climbing the rigging sounded like fun.

Hand over hand through the rat-lines they clambered. The rope ladder swayed in the breeze and the boys hung on with all their might. The deck lay far below and the ship rocked alarmingly. Up in the rigging the sails flapped with a deafening roar.

Finally, they reached the crow's nest and scanned the ocean, and sure enough they saw a sail in the distance. They were heading towards it at a fast pace and it was coming straight for them. Al put the telescope to his eye.

He could now see that the ship was a familiar, two-masted brigantine. Al studied the flag. It was a Jolly Roger.

"It's Blacktooth!" he cried. "At two o'clock!" He fixed his eyes on *The Revenge*

and noticed the flash of another telescope. "They've seen us!"

Gunner had no desire to fight Blacktooth again, so he jibed *The Booty* and came about. They ran before the faster craft, but were too slow. Gunner's old ship had no chance.

As the skies darkened and a rainy squall

burst upon them, so did Blacktooth. His ship soon came close by. His longer range guns told Gunner and his crew that Blacktooth had no desire to rob them, but only to sink them, for a shot just missed their bows.

The second shot fell behind, but the third

shot went through the hull. The fourth disabled the main mast.

With *The Booty* disabled and sinking and a storm approaching, Blacktooth tacked to port and sailed away.

The Booty's crew set to bailing. "Get the mast down!" cried Gunner. "If that storm hits us, the sails will fill and it'll sink us in a minute."

Jack and Al helped cut the rigging lines on the mast and it toppled into the sea just as the storm hit. Then everyone bailed for their lives as the ship tossed and pitched. Great storm clouds broke overhead and waves smashed them. Still, they bailed and worked against all odds to keep *The Booty* afloat.

As *The Booty* listed lower in the water, Jack rushed to Al's side. "Look," he said, "over there. It's a volcano sticking out of the ocean." He pointed. "See the smoke?"

"And a cliff," shouted Al, squinting

through the raging waves and pouring rain. Land appeared to leeward and strange larval rocks emerged through the mist of smoke and rain. “That rock looks like a big skull,” said Jack, pointing further south.

Gunner came up behind them.

"Land!" cried Jack. "We're saved!"

Gunner peered through the storm. "That's not a safe place," he said. "Keep bailing and pray the currents carry us past that dreaded island."

But the currents pushed the disabled ship closer and closer to the skull rock until the grinding of wood on rock told everyone that the ship was hard aground.

"We won't drown, thank heavens," said Al.

"Drowning would have been better," replied Gunner, "for we are shipwrecked on Ghost Island."

Clues to the Puzzle

Each symbol on page 82 stands for a letter of the alphabet. Since the code on the back of the cameo spells 'Princess Halimeda Alleric', you already know what some of the letters are. Use this knowledge to work out what the code in the diary says.

If you still need help decoding the message, visit www.dragonbloodpirates.co.uk

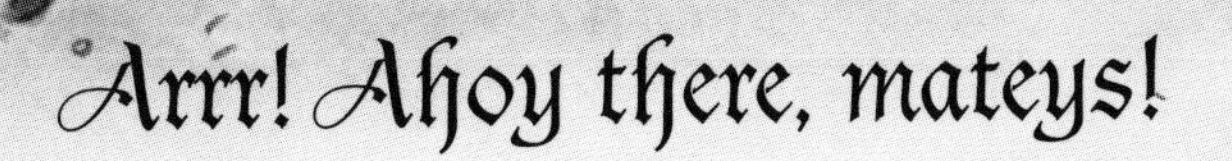

Hoist the sails and drop the anchor: ye have some treasure to find!

One swashbucklin' reader will win a haul of booty, including an Xbox console and games and an iTunes voucher, and twelve runners up will win a Dragon Blood Pirates booty bag.

For a chance to win, ye must dare to unearth the treasure using the Dragon Blood Islands map from *Death Diamond* (also available to download at www.dragonbloodpirates.co.uk), and the six big pirate stickers that are inserted in every book.

Each of the six Dragon Blood Pirates books contains a clue revealing an island protected by a dastardly pirate, and a sticker of the pirate to place on your map. When ye have solved the six clues, and have placed the six stickers, there will remain only one island, where the pirate booty be.

To win, enter online at
www.dragonbloodpirates.co.uk

Or send your name, address and the name of the island where the treasure lies to:

Dragon Blood Pirates Treasure Hunt
338 Euston Road, London NW1 3BH

Best o'luck, me hearties!

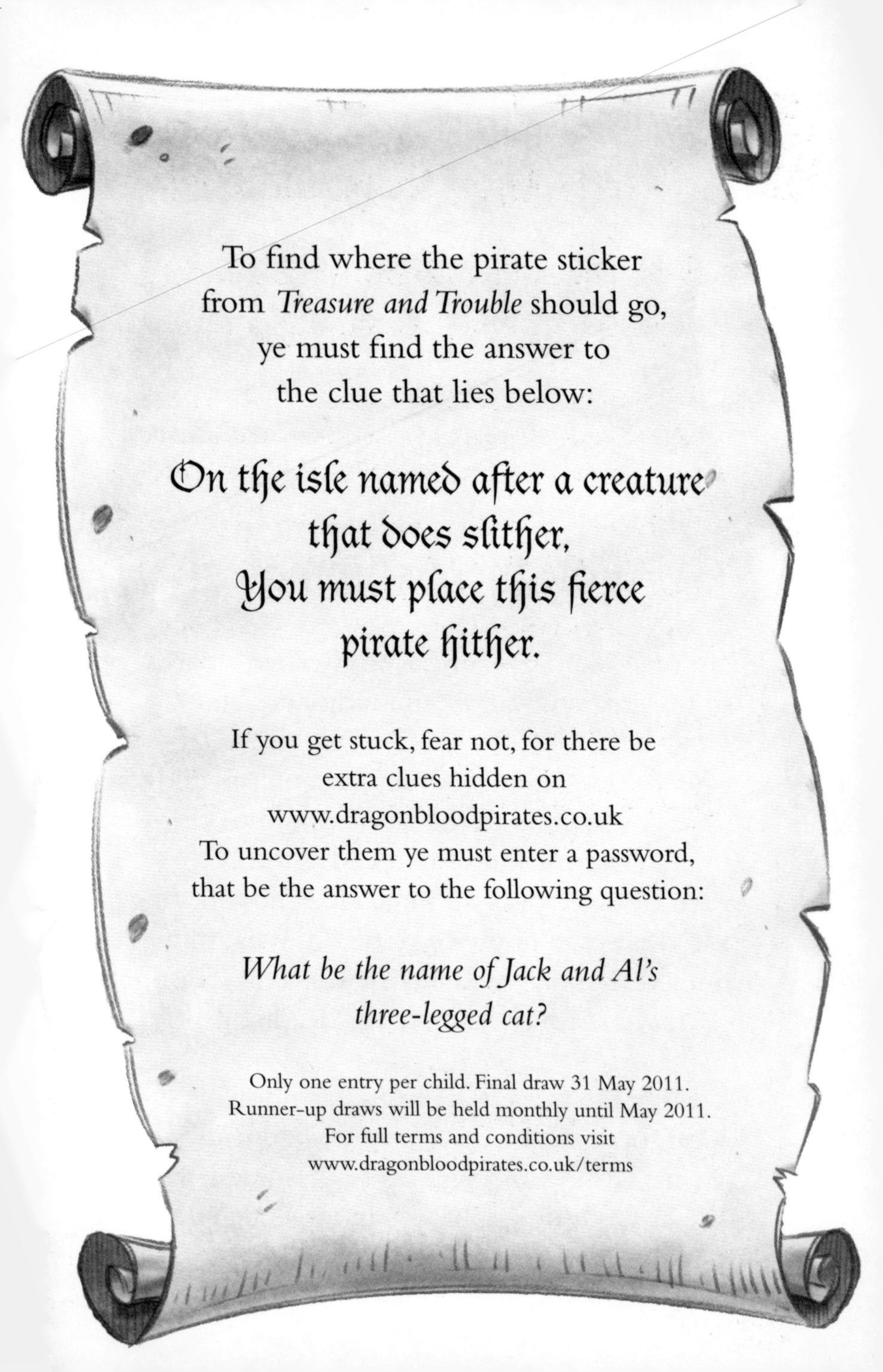
To find where the pirate sticker
from *Treasure and Trouble* should go,
ye must find the answer to
the clue that lies below:
On the isle named after a creature
that does slither,
You must place this fierce
pirate hither.
If you get stuck, fear not, for there be
extra clues hidden on
www.dragonbloodpirates.co.uk
To uncover them ye must enter a password,
that be the answer to the following question:
*What be the name of Jack and Al's
three-legged cat?*
Only one entry per child. Final draw 31 May 2011.
Runner-up draws will be held monthly until May 2011.
For full terms and conditions visit
www.dragonbloodpirates.co.uk/terms

Ahoy there shipmates!

To reel in amazin' pirate booty, steer smartly towards www.dragonbloodpirates.co.uk

Ye'll find games, downloads, activities and sneak previews of the latest swashbucklin' Dragon Blood Pirates adventures. Learn how to speak all pirate-like, how to find out what type of pirate ye be, an' what pirate games ye can play with yer mates! This treasure trove is a sure feast fer yer deadlights!

Only the bravest an' heartiest amon' ye can become a true scurvy dog, so don't ye miss a thing and sign up to yer newsletter at www.dragonbloodpirates.co.uk!

Don't ye miss book six in the

Dragon Blood Pirates

series!

Turn the page and shiver yer timbers
with a slice of the next high-seas adventure...

Ghost Island

Al was dreaming he was at home watching TV. The smell of a roast dinner cooking in the oven and the comfort of his couch in the lounge room made him smile. Jack, his best friend, came through the front door, sat down beside him and gave him a playful punch on the shoulder. Then he punched him harder.

Al's dream evaporated. He awoke to find Jack shaking him. It took Al a second to

realise he wasn't at home but in the main cabin of the pirate ship *The Booty*, where it was dark and damp. Al's stomach rumbled. He was really hungry.

Around him the crew of *The Booty* snored, deep in sleep, exhausted after hours of bailing and fighting at sea. They had nearly sunk in a storm, but had been washed ashore on Ghost Island.

Al's sister, Hally, was sleeping heavily in the corner beside him. Snakeboot the cat was curled up beside Hally, but his ever-watchful purple eyes stared purposefully at the cabin door. He twitched his tail, fully alert.

"Jack, what are you doing?" said Al. "I was so happy sleeping."

"Listen," said Jack.

Al listened. He could hear the lap of waves on the hull and the creaking of the ship as it shifted on the sand.

"What? I can't hear anything unusual."

A sudden thump came from above. Then another. The cabin door shook and a ghostly cry raised the hair on Al's arms. "Is it a sea bird?" he asked.

"No," said Jack. His face was pale. "Someone's out there, calling for us."

The terrifying cry came again from

just outside the door. Al jumped to his feet, opened the cabin door a crack and peered out. The first sunrays had tinged the morning fog red. Clouds of blood-coloured vapour drifted around the wrecked *Booty*. In the steaming mist Al thought he saw a man, bent and wavering in the strange light. Then, closer to the door, another man turned to stare at the boys. His face was a rotting mask, with lumps of flesh peeling from his skull. The apparition raised a skeletal hand and pointed. "Snakebroooot," he exclaimed as he spied the three-legged cat standing at Al's feet.

Al shut the door with a bang. "Am I still asleep?" he cried. "Jack, pinch me!"

"Unfortunately you're awake," said Jack. "I saw them too. I think Gunner was right. There *are* ghosts on this island."

The boys stepped over Slicer, the cook, who was still sleeping, and went to the

cabin window. The sun was cutting through the fog, revealing a skull-like rock jutting out of the sea. Lava had once flowed from the towering volcano that loomed over the island. Forbidding caverns in the rock made the eye sockets and the nose. The crooked teeth plunged into the water and waves lapped around the jaw. "It sure is a spooky-looking place," said Al. "Maybe it was just the fog playing tricks."

"The fog can't say 'Snakeboot'," said Jack.

One by one the crew woke up. Mahoot, the cabin boy, was rubbing the sleep from his eyes. Al went over to him. "Mahoot," he whispered, "are there really ghosts on this island?"

Mahoot's eyes went wide. He nodded. "Shhh," he said. "They are the ghosts of Vicious Victor's pirates. Don't mention them. Even saying the name 'Vicious Victor' is unlucky." The words had just left his

mouth when footsteps thumped on the deck outside. Mahoot paled.

Slicer jumped to his feet and clutched his sword.

Mozzy, the bosun, shook Captain Gunner awake. "Captain," he squealed, "they've found us already!"

Captain Gunner sat up. He, too, heard the clumping of ghostly feet on the deck. Then a voice echoed eerily through the cabin. "Come out! Come out and join us."

All the pirates ran to the back of the cabin and cowered against the wall furthest from the door. Captain Gunner picked up a musket and pointed it at the door. "You're not gunner come in here!" he shouted.

The commotion woke Hally, who looked around in fright. "What's happening?" she asked.

"Vicious Victor's ghost crew is on board," said Captain Gunner, "and if they get to us

they're gunner take our bodies."

Jack and Al looked at each other in disbelief.

"Ghosts?" Hally shrieked, bursting into tears and running to her brother's side. "Al, I want to go home *now*. I don't want to play pirates. Please, please take me home."

Al fingered the old iron key in his pocket. The rusty key unlocked the magical sea trunk back in his attic at home, at number five Drake Drive. He wished he was there right now, eating a nice roast dinner and watching TV. But he, Hally and Jack had made the decision to come to the Dragon Blood Islands to search for the Dragon Blood Sabre. There was no going home unless they could find the magical portal back to the twenty-first

century. Besides, it was Snakeboot who normally showed them the way home. Now the cat just sat by the cabin door while the ghosts called his name.

"I'm sorry, but I don't know how to get home, Hally," said Al, patting his sister's hand.

The Ghosts

Time passed and the tide came in, leaving a channel of water between Ghost Island and *The Booty*. Strangely, the ghost invaders no longer tapped at the cabin door or haunted the ship. But even though all was quiet, the superstitious pirates shivered in dread and the tension in the cabin mounted.

"If we stay in here we'll die of hunger," said Al. "It's either the ghosts or starvation. There's no choice. We have to go out."

Captain Gunner stared at Al. "You're not gunner go out there," he ordered.

"If you let Al and me go," reasoned Jack, "we can get food. We're kids. Ghost pirates probably wouldn't want to possess kids. We might be safe where you might not be. It's worth a try."

"And I really want to look for the sabre," added Al. "This is why we wanted you to bring us to Ghost Island. The sabre is supposed to be here."

"I'd much prefer you stayed safe," said Gunner, "but if you are fixed on the idea I can't stop you. Still, I'd feel better if we put it to the vote." All nodded in agreement. "All those in favour of the boys going out, say 'aye'."

"If *they* get possessed it might save a few of us," said one pirate from the back of the cabin.

"We're all doomed anyway," said another

one. "Probably best for them to die first."

This started a general argument and after several minutes of heated debate, the pirates voted in favour of the boys leaving the ship.

Al and Jack went to the door. "Are you going to come with us, Mahoot?" asked Jack.

Mahoot paled, then bravely stepped forward. "I'm not leaving you to go out

alone. You might need me," he answered. "Besides, I want the famous sabre returned to Sabre Island too."

"I'm coming as well," said Hally. "I don't think a pirate ghost would want me. I can't imagine a pirate wanting to be a little girl."

"Blinkin' barnacles, no!" agreed the pirates in the cabin.

Snakeboot was the first to bound through

the open cabin door, followed by Jack, Al, Hally and Mahoot. The door shut with a bang behind them. Fearfully, they peered around the decks. The ghosts were nowhere to be seen. "Do you think the high tide's keeping them away?" asked Jack.

"Pirates can't swim, so you might be right," replied Al. "Even so, we'll try our luck ashore."

They lowered themselves overboard on ropes and waded through the shallow waters to the beach. Al held Snakeboot high so he wouldn't get wet. As soon as Snakeboot's paws touched the sand, he took off down the beach away from the skull rock. The volcano rumbled ominously and the island shook. The hilly sand dunes behind the beach hissed menacingly as grains of sand slid down their steep slopes.

Dragon Blood Pirates
www.dragonbloodpirates.co.uk
Have ye the courage to brave the stormy seas?
Dragon Blood Pirates
Q: What did the pirate say when he had a heart attack?
A: Arr! Me hearty!
ORCHARD BOOKS
Not suitable for children under 36 months due to small parts
© Orchard Books 2010